The Boy Who Stopped Time

The Boy Who Stopped Time

Anthony Taber

MARGARET K. MCELDERRY BOOKS · NEW YORK

Maxwell Macmillan Canada · Toronto

Maxwell Macmillan International · New York · Oxford · Singapore · Sydney

Margaret K. McElderry Books, Macmillan Publishing Company, 866 Third Avenue, New York, NY 10022

Maxwell Macmillan Canada, Inc., 1200 Eglinton Avenue East, Suite 200, Don Mills, Ontario M3C 3N1

Macmillan Publishing Company is part of the Maxwell Communication Group of Companies.

First edition   Printed in the United States of America

2   4   6   8   10   9   7   5   3   1

The text of this book is set in Stempel Schneidler.

The illustrations are rendered in pencil on paper.

Library of Congress Cataloging-in-Publication Data

Taber, Anthony. The boy who stopped time / Anthony Taber. — 1st ed.   p.   cm.

Summary: Julian stops the pendulum from swinging on the clock and has a marvelous adventure while the rest of the world is suspended in time.

ISBN 0-689-50460-8

[1. Time — Fiction.   2. Clocks and watches — Fiction.]   I. Title.   PZ7.T1127Bo   1993   [E] — dc20   92-398

FOR JULIAN

NO MATTER how much fun he was having, every night at 7:30, when the clock on the living room wall went *ding-dong,* Julian had to go to bed.

One summer evening, just before bedtime, Julian asked his mom if he could stay up late to watch a special TV show. "No, Julian," she said. "You need your rest more than you need that show. When the big hand gets to the six, it's off to bed with you." She left the living room to tuck in his little sister, AnnaRose.

Julian watched the clock's pendulum swing back and forth until the big hand
slid past the five. Then he went to the window. Outside, his father was piling
stones in the yard. And from his sister's bedroom he heard his mother begin a
lullaby. Julian suddenly had a wonderful idea.

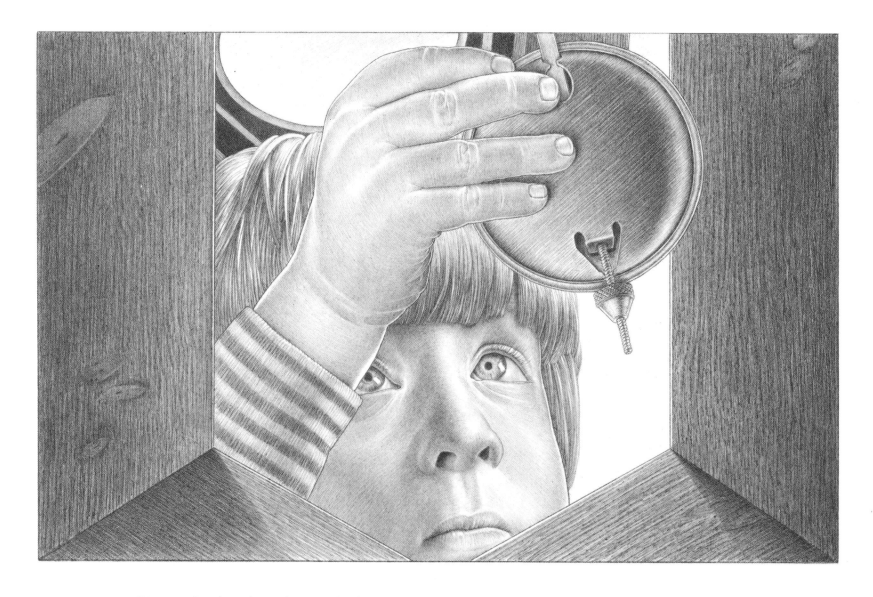

He pushed a chair beneath the clock, then climbed up and opened the clock's face. He took a deep breath…and stopped the pendulum. A strange hush fell over the house.

He closed the clock and looked around. The TV screen was silent. On it, a cowboy about to mount his horse stood motionless, with one foot in the stirrup and the other on the ground. Something was wrong. Julian waited, but the cowboy didn't move. Julian hopped off the chair and tried the other channels. There was no motion or sound on any of them.

He tiptoed down the hall to his sister's room. There in the shadows was his mom, leaning over AnnaRose's crib. Her mouth was open as if she were singing, and AnnaRose was smiling up at her. Everything looked perfectly normal, except his mom and his sister were both as still and quiet as statues. Julian backed out of the room, amazed at what he had done, and ran outside.

He found his dad with his arms outstretched by the rock pile, his eyes fixed on a big rock he had just thrown. Julian called to him but got no reply. Looking at his dad made Julian feel guilty. He had not intended to have *everything* stop, only the clock. Maybe he should start the clock again, even though he would have to go to bed.

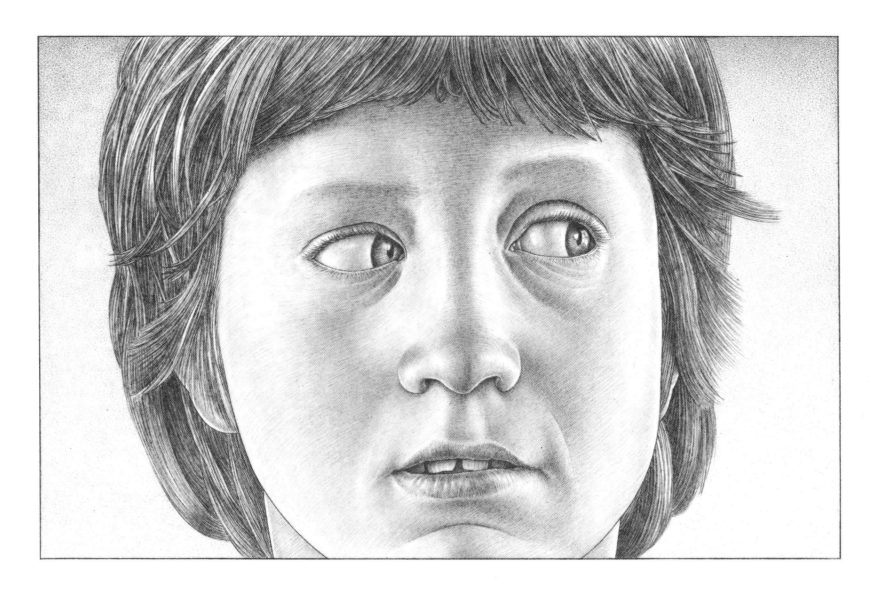

But on the way back to the house he thought of not having to go to bed. The more he thought about it the better he liked the idea. If he didn't start the clock he never had to go to bed again. So…

Instead of going inside he walked slowly around the house, fascinated by the eerie stillness. On the other side of the lawn, he found Shadow, the family dog, in frozen pursuit of a big gray fox. He stopped to feel the fox's silky ears.

Around the front of the house he discovered dozens of birds stalled in midair between the feeder and surrounding trees. He reached up, delighted to run his fingers lightly over the birds' soft feathers without their flying away.

Down by the creek that edged their land, he encountered a magnificent buck deer. It was twice his height, with a huge rack of antlers. Julian had to use a stepladder from the shed to reach its back.

Up there he felt like king of all he saw, and he wished he could make the deer move from the creek and race over the countryside. He looked at his house and his father by the stone pile. He could still go anywhere and do anything he wanted. He decided to take his bike up the driveway to the main road, where he was strictly forbidden to go.

Before leaving, he stopped at the house, gave his mom a secret kiss good-bye,
and took some cookies for the trip.

He pedaled fearlessly out onto the main road and didn't stop until he was almost a mile away, at the first intersection. He had never been this far on his own before. Then he decided to go a little farther toward the town to look at a car standing still on the road. From that car he went to the next and then the next, studying the faces inside. Nothing and no one was moving. He went all the way to the town bridge.

On the town bridge he stared down at a rowing team, they and their boat motionless on the water below. Home was far behind him now, and he felt very small and alone in the strange stillness.

Before him the silent town waited. A few blocks from the bridge Julian
suddenly recognized Russell's Auto Repair, where his dad had his car fixed and
where Julian's buddy, Dick, worked. He called to him as he rolled up. Dick
would really be surprised to see him all by himself in town on his bike. Then
he remembered. Dick wouldn't be able to talk either, and wouldn't even know
he was there.

He continued up the street and stopped at the fire station, drawn by the great engines standing in a row. He cautiously opened the door of a big hook and ladder, expecting someone to come out of the station to chase him away. But no one did, and he pulled himself up onto the cool leather of the driver's seat and sat for a long while behind the wheel, wishing his legs were long enough to reach the pedals.

He went deeper into the silence of the town to visit the toy department in Woolworth's. For a while he forgot the silence.

Julian stopped at the library next. It was still hard to read by himself. He wished Miss Bruning, the children's librarian, could help as she had many times before.

Then he visited the Napoli Pizzeria, where his father sometimes took him for a special treat. But no one could give him a slice of pizza to eat.

He went to the movie theater, but the picture wasn't moving, and the silence and stillness crept into him. He felt sleepy and dozed off. Julian didn't know how long he had slept because when he woke up everything was exactly the same. Then he remembered how he had stopped the clock so he wouldn't have to go to sleep.

Listening to the silence within himself, Julian pedaled to the town park. He looked at all the children frozen in their play. Now his feeling of silence started to become a feeling of sadness, and he knew that he wanted to go home.

He took the back road home. Cows and horses stood motionless in the fields, and high above, an airplane hung in the sky. He was very tired when he arrived and very happy to find everything waiting for him just as he had left it.

He put his bike away, went inside, peeked in on his mom, climbed up on the chair, and started the clock pendulum swinging. His mother's lullaby began again. He got down and silently returned the chair to its place. The lullaby ended, the clock went *ding-dong,* and his mother said, "It's time, Julian."

He took one last look out the window. His father was throwing another stone on the pile. Down by the creek, the deer had gone, and over the meadow honeybees gathered nectar in the evening sun. Julian smiled to himself and quietly went to bed.